The Professor's History

By Claire Messud

When the World Was Steady

The Last Life

The Hunters

The Emperor's Children

Claire Messud

The Professor's History

PICADOR SHOTS

First published 2006 by Picador
an imprint of Pan Macmillan Ltd
Pan Macmillan, 20 New Wharf Road, London N1 9RR
Basingstoke and Oxford
Associated companies throughout the world
www.panmacmillan.com

ISBN-13: 978-0-330-44577-1
ISBN-10: 0-330-44577-4

1 3 5 7 9 8 6 4 2

A CIP catalogue record for this book is available from
the British Library.

Typeset by Intype Libra Ltd
Printed and bound in Great Britain by
Mackays of Chatham plc, Chatham, Kent

THE PROFESSOR WIPED HIS forehead with his handkerchief, and then took off his glasses and wiped them too, fussing over their wire arms and squinting in the vast light. The train spat clouds of grit and steam as it hauled itself back into motion and off, towards the naked mountains.

Around him, there was no station to speak of, just an empty shack with no door, and a jarring French railroad sign pinned to the wall, its fancy blue letters neatly, but dustily, announcing CAS-SAIGNE.

The professor—a slight, weathered man in his mid-forties, with a small forehead and a Gallic profile, carefully attired in a cream linen suit with a crisp straw hat—was not a man to look absurd: even alone, at the side of the endless ladder of the

I

track, in the middle of the scrubby foothills, he managed to retain some of his composure. When he saw, in the distance, a man swaddled in a burnous, he did not call out. As befit a Frenchman, and especially a Frenchman so long in Algeria, he waited. The Arab made his way, unhurried, towards him.

Their exchange was terse, conducted in a pidgin that allowed each the room of his own language—for the words that mattered most. The professor was headed to Necmaria, a village in the foothills of the Dahra, midway between Algiers and Oran. He needed food, a couple of mules and a guide. It would be possible, said the local man, but would involve waiting, and leaving at dawn, aiming to traverse the fifty or so kilometres in a single, exhausting day. The man would not go himself, but his brother, who possessed two mules, could perhaps lead the expedition. They would take the man's son, a boy of about fifteen: there was strength in numbers. Tomorrow was possible. Tomorrow it would be. The professor could sleep the night with the brother's family—theirs was a larger house, the provision more adequate for a foreigner.

The Arab did not ask, then, by the train tracks, why the professor wanted to go to Necmaria. He thought he knew. It was an uncomfortable history between them, Arab and Frenchman, better not made explicit. Both were aware that the only reason for a Frenchman to travel to Necmaria was to see the caves of Dahra. A history better left buried.

In fact, the professor was working on a book. A strange thing to do, in the mountains of North Africa, in the middle of a war, when metropolitan France teetered (the line was so close to Paris that the troops were sent to the front in taxis), and all Europe was confusion and fear. The professor should not, for so many reasons, have been pursuing these stories, ugly and old as they were. If anything, he knew it was a time to be looking forward, beyond the war. He was driven, though, by something he had read, a sentence in the letters of a colonel. Bent over yellowing pages in the city library, intent upon his research, he had unearthed the letters of St Arnaud, and with them the promise, or threat, of historical discovery: an act, an immense act, had passed unrecorded. A glimmer in a dusty corner, it drew him back, and back, and then, eventually, out of the city library and out of the city itself. Silently, the professor had grown convinced that this history was relevant—or even, when the glimmer was at its most insistent, crucial—to the current conflict. He carried the leather-bound volume of letters with him at all times, like a prayer-book. But he knew enough not to discuss his work with anyone.

Mustafa, the local man's brother, was not as restrained as his sibling. That evening, as they sat down to supper by the quivering fire, beneath a candy-coloured mackerel dusk, Mustafa asked why. He was entitled: they were his mules, and he was to lead them. But the question brought, nonetheless, a silence in which only the bleating of goats and the sharp reports of the burning kindling gave answer.

'I have business with the *caid*,' answered the professor at last. He mopped at his stew with grave concentration and chewed on his bread. The firelight was reflected in his glasses, and the other men could not see his eyes.

'What business would that be?' asked Mustafa, playing his fingers in his beard. 'He is not—may Allah forgive me if I am mistaken—not a man of any importance to your government.'

'I am not a government official,' said the professor, suddenly weary. 'I am a historian. I record history.'

'The caves,' said Ibrahim, Mustafa's nephew, only now understanding. 'You wish to visit the caves of Dahra.'

The professor would neither confirm nor deny it, and Mustafa and Ibrahim knew it was so.

'Will you want us to stay, while you do your business?' asked Mustafa. 'Or will you not be coming back to Cassaigne?'

The professor looked up, seemingly surprised that the wash of night had closed in around them, carried on the waves of chill air. 'I don't know,' he said. 'I will decide tomorrow.'

The professor did not sleep well. He felt

oppressed by the secret music of other people's slumber—these exhalations and whisperings somehow more alien for being Muslim—and the earthen floor of the house poked bony and cold into his spine. Although very tired, or perhaps because of it, he found his mind restless, his imagination conjuring scenarios he could not wish to contemplate. It occurred to him that he did not know what tribe his hosts belonged to; nor did he know how long they had been settled in Cassaigne or, indeed, been settled at all. He did not know what to expect of Necmaria; nor could he gauge the relationship between Mustafa's people and those of that village. And where might the allegiances of the people of Rabelais fall?

The professor, in following the account in the colonel's letter, proposed to move onwards from Necmaria to Rabelais, a distance of a further hundred kilometres. There were caves near Rabelais also, and although their name—the caves of Sbéhas—did not carry the same weight of dread as did that of Necmaria, it soon would, if the colonel had written truthfully, and if the professor was to convey that truth to the world. In both cases, Necmaria and Rabelais, the story of the caves was not only a tale of Europeans and the natives: there were tribal tales, too, of betrayal and unsavoury rewards. The professor did not know enough. As he sought to align his limbs to the ungenerous curve of the ground, as he drew his coarse blanket closer around him and inhaled its greasy stink, he recognized that he did not know the full meaning or consequences of his work, that he was a learned man who knew nothing outside the walls of the city library. For a long time he lay, cold and sweating in his papoose, eyes open to the blackness, watching without seeing and measuring the darkness.

The journey was long. Wakened before dawn by the call of the village *muezzin*, the professor performed his ablutions separately from the Muslims and busied himself with his notebooks while they prayed. In the city, despite the subjects of his research, he was conscious of these rituals only as a charming Oriental flavour to his adopted land. He found it at once embarrassing and miraculous to be at their centre, among the men and their families and their prayers in a guttural language, as if he had stumbled upon a naked woman for the first time and could not define his response to her shimmering flesh.

The mules were loaded as the sun rose. The professor was to sit upon one, while the other bore his case and the supplies. He was surprised at the pace set by Mustafa and Ibrahim, who walked behind and flicked, intermittently, at the baggage mule with a switch. There was no sound but this, their steps and the ticking of insects. None of them spoke. The route they followed was along the foothills, the mountains rising always alongside them. The terrain, although unsteady and, for the professor—whose back ached already from the night before—uncomfortable, was not difficult. The mules were dogged and unfaltering in their progress, but Mustafa and Ibrahim seemed to find them too slow. They yelled at the blinking beasts, who merely flicked their ears and did not change their pace. In the course of the day, the troupe paused only for prayers and a hasty *casse-croute*, consumed in the paltry shade of a wild-limbed shrub.

Twilight hovered as they glimpsed the cluster of houses that was Necmaria. In the gloom, the red dirt walls of the habitation glowed like embers. The professor's eyes were heavy-lidded, his glasses, unwiped, so smeared with dust that he could barely see. But the proximity of rest, of the long-imagined destination, revived him, and he straightened his frame as best he could. He made an unspoken effort to reassert his European authority, remembering that he commanded the two Arabs and not they him, a fact which their progress had served to deny. But it was Mustafa who approached the first fire they came upon and asked for the *caid*'s house; and Ibrahim who helped the professor, bent to the shape of his mule, to dismount.

In so small a village, the *caid*'s house was not difficult to find. Two storeys high, it loomed over the others, its heavy wooden doors studded and bolted to the street, and the high slivers in the walls that were its windows unlit.

Mustafa and Ibrahim had called four times before they heard the bolts shifting angrily on the far side of the door. It opened just a little, revealing a boy younger than Ibrahim, unbearded, bearing a torch. Alarmed, he proceeded anyway with the formal greetings in a tremulous tone.

'We wish to see the *caid*,' explained Mustafa. 'This man has business with the *caid*.'

The professor stepped forward, into the pool of light. He spoke in French, and the boy did not understand. He tried again, his Arabic slow and careful. 'I am a historian. I am here to discuss history with the *caid*.'

'The *caid* is not here,' said the boy. 'He is from home on a journey of some weeks. His steward, my father, is with him. You are welcome, but I can offer you little.' He opened the door wide to the gloomy passage, at the end of which spread the courtyard, where a small fire was visible. 'Come in.'

Ibrahim handed the professor his case, and the

two men from Cassaigne made as if to withdraw. The professor was suddenly uneasy: he had not expected to be in the hands of a child, and he feared both that the expedition would prove fruitless, and that he would not find a way back from Necmaria. The city seemed very far away, and his worth in this bare world slight. Elsewhere, he remembered, there was war.

Mustafa sensed his confusion, and for a moment drew close enough to touch him. 'We will sleep by the first fire, on the edge of the village. If you need me, send the boy.' Then they were gone.

'Who remains, in the absence of the *caid*?' asked the professor, as the youth slid the iron bolts between them and the street.

'I do.' The boy coughed. 'My name is Menouira.' The cough was an ellipsis that the professor understood: now within the walls, he could hear the sounds of living, the muffled ring of voices and occasional laughter. The women— the *caid*'s wife, perhaps, and daughters; the boy's mother; the servant girls—were in residence, but the professor would not see them.

The courtyard was encircled by arcades, and a dead fountain squatted at its centre, a mosaic trough that shone dry beneath the stars. There were doorways in the cloistered corridors, but all were shut. The boy stoked the fire and crouched down beside it.

'This is a house with many rooms,' he said, 'but I fear you will have to sleep by the fire with me. The *caid*, in his wisdom, does not leave me the keys. I cannot open any of the doors.'

Even Menouira's food, it transpired, came not from the house stores but from his cousins in the village. The women were locked in their quarters like penned sheep, with food and water and lamplight enough for the duration of the *caid*'s absence.

'But what if something should delay his return?' asked the professor, amazed, picking at his meagre half of Menouira's supper and thinking of Mustafa and Ibrahim, warm and plentifully fed, on the edge of the village. 'Surely this is a dangerous way for the *caid* to leave his affairs?'

The boy's face registered nothing. 'The *caid*, in his wisdom . . .' he began again. There was a circle of laughter in the walls, as if the women had heard and made mock.

'What sort of man is the *caid*?' the professor asked.

'He is a very learned man. A wealthy man. A just man.'

'Of what age?'

'His beard is white, but he is not so old.'

'And did he build this house?'

'His grandfather built this house.'

'And his grandfather also owned the land?'

'He was given the land,' said the boy, 'by your government. By the government of France. It is a line of *caid*s, always on good terms with the French. The land belongs to him on all sides, as far as you can see on a bright day.'

'And can you see to the cave—the cave of the Ouled Riah, in the Dahra?' asked the professor.

Menouira was suddenly wary. 'You can see to

the cave, although you cannot distinguish it from here,' he said, and was quiet.

'Were the *caid*'s people in the cave?' persisted the Frenchman, knowing the answer was everything.

'No,' said the boy, sullen now. 'The Ouled Riah are not the *caid*'s people.'

'And the people of Necmaria?' continued the professor.

'They are of the Ouled Riah, perhaps half of them.'

'And yourself?'

'My mother's family, yes. But not my father. Nor I.' The boy poked angrily at the flames with a stick, and turned his body sideways.

This was the story of the caves of Dahra, as the professor knew it: on 19 June 1845, around a thousand people—men, women and children—concealed themselves from the French troops in the cave, along with their animals and belongings. It was a cave the Ouled Riah had used for generations, father to son: a resting place, a hiding place.

The times, a mere fifteen years since the end of the nation's occupation by the Turks, were uncertain; and the French were as jumpy as the tribes were hostile. The Marechal Pelissier—a brutal, straightforward, awkward man—found that his men, on approaching the refuge, were fired upon by the Ouled Riah. And in his anger, Pelissier ordered that the entrance to their hideout be blocked by fire, and burning torches thrown inside.

The troops stood by in the moonlight, while the screams of the families and animals echoed in the caverns like the laughter of the *caid*'s womenfolk in the house walls, and the rocks burst in the heat. For a long time, they did nothing. At dawn, as the anguish abated, Pelissier deemed his military goal accomplished. The soldiers—not hastily—doused the conflagration and removed the debris from the mouth of the cave. Under Pelissier's orders, the men then helped the choking survivors to safety, a mere hundred or so, those who had lain closest to the ground and hoarded the air from the dying. Their skin was

blackened with smoke, and their eyes were
streaming, their wails of mourning trapped in
their lungs for lack of oxygen. Battered and hum-
bled, these survivors stayed in Necmaria, making
their lives in the shadow of their deaths, bearing
their children before the monument of their holo-
caust.

The caves harboured another story too.
Pelissier and his men had been seeking the tribe of
the Ouled Riah, to conquer and adopt them in the
name of France. But they could not discover their
encampment. Nor would they have, not knowing
about the existence of the cave, which was as well
hidden as that of the Forty Thieves. But Pelissier
unearthed, in the form of the *khalifa* of another
tribe, his open Sesame. Feuding with the Ouled
Riah, this *khalifa* cleaved to the French. He clear-
ly explained the location of the hiding place (this
knowledge had been passed on, father to son,
for generations); and when the troops still could
not find it, the *khalifa* dispatched his attendants.
These loyal men revealed the cave to Pelissier and

his battalion, leading them to it from above so that they could approach undisclosed.

The *khalifa* was well rewarded for his pains: he was named *caid* of Necmaria, and given the land around the village as far as the eye could see, for his own benefit and that of his descendants. A stone's throw from the site of his treachery, the *caid* raised his family in prosperity and ease, in the warmth of the French embrace; he ruled, and his offspring ruled, over the tattered remnants of his enemies.

'Will you take me to the cave tomorrow?' asked the professor.

'If you wish.' Menouira did not look at him: he was pacing the arcades in search of an extra blanket for the professor. As he handed it to him, he said: 'You are the first Frenchman in my lifetime to want to visit the cave. You shouldn't have come. It is better left buried.'

The women's laughter carilloned in the walls.

In the morning, Menouira and the professor

breakfasted with Menouira's relatives in the village. Under the clear sky, the professor could see the land dropping away on the far side of the *caid*'s house, an immense, roseate plain dotted with trees, and sheep and goats, and the hillside nubbed by the early shoots of crops, patterns of green in the red earth. The glistening mirror of Oued Zerifa zigzagged its way across the land. The *caid*'s triumph was glorious.

Mustafa and Ibrahim found him there.

'What of your business?' asked Mustafa in a voice that seemed to the Frenchman no longer friendly, but sneering. 'Will you go to the cave without the *caid*?'

'I intend to.'

'It is perhaps better that the *caid* is absent,' Mustafa continued. 'These, my brothers, are the people to whom the tragedy belongs. It is their place.' He smiled, and Menouira and the others smiled also, as if this were a happy fact. 'And will you return to Cassaigne? We shall wait.'

The professor hesitated. 'I would like to go

on tomorrow,' he said. 'I hoped to go on to Rabelais.' He paused. 'Will you take me there?'

The group fell silent.

'I have important business in Rabelais,' he insisted. 'If you will not take me, perhaps someone else?'

'It is two days' journey. Why did you not tell me before?' asked Mustafa. 'We would need another mule. We would need food.'

'This could be arranged,' said another man. 'If you so wish it.'

'In Europe, there is a war,' said the professor, as if this were an explanation. 'I must get to Rabelais. It is important.'

'We will take you,' said Mustafa.

'I will rent you a mule,' said Menouira's cousin.

'I can provide food,' said another. And the deal was struck.

Menouira and the professor set off to the cave near noon. The entrance itself was invisible from Necmaria, hidden among a cluster of coppery boulders. The path Menouira took, along the ridge of the slight escarpment, snaked outwards in an 's' from the village, dipped only to the *oued*, which they crossed on stepping stones, and rose again to bring the pair to their destination from above, just as Pelissier had been brought. The descent to the mouth was awkward: twice the professor slid, the second time scraping his hands as he fell, knocking his glasses from his nose. Menouira retrieved them and attempted to brush the red earth from the professor's sullied suit, to no avail. The dirt clung in the creases of the fabric like streaks of dried blood.

The professor, in his research, had not been able to picture the cave. He had not realized that a small stream would trickle so carelessly into its mouth; nor that the overhanging rocks would reach so ominously downwards, their tentacles like pointing fingers; nor that the breadth of the coloured plain would lie, like an invitation and a promise, at his feet.

When they entered it, the cave was not what the professor had, till now, understood by the word: strictly speaking a riverbed, it was comprised of a single gallery through the rock, without branches or smaller tributaries, wavering only slightly in its downward course. The *oued*, once underground, became a floor of muck rather than a river. The walls sweated, dripped their moisture like irregular footfalls into the mud. As Menouira led the way, the professor realized that the cave did not open out into any chamber, and at times, his elbows, outstretched, measured its width. There were moments when the torch-smoke wavered upwards into the darkness without illuminating any ceiling, so high was the gallery; at other points, Menouira's arm would reach backwards to him, urging his body into a stoop, as the passage dwindled to less than a metre tall. Throughout, their little light cast fantastic shadows, as of contorted figures beckoning along the wet walls, made surprisingly pale and uneven by accretions of guano. Hollow recesses offered the only variation: some high, others at the level of the men's knees; some rounded, as if sanded by craftsmen, others jagged enough to cut.

The professor stopped, after a time, and

watched Menouira's torch diminish in front of him. He turned a full circle, breathing deeply. He fought the pressure of his heart in the cave of his ribs, the force of history like a life around him. A thousand men, women and children, with their animals and belongings, peopled the space: hunched in crevices, pressed against the moist walls, their cheeks to the cold stone, their buttocks and arms and feet meeting in the subterranean night. The animals lowed, the young women nursed their infants, soothing them with rhythmic words, clucking at the children who clung to their legs, up to their ankles in mud. There was no place to lie, no square metre any of these ghosts could claim for their own, huddled against one another and their beasts, cramped and stinking, giving off a sour heat. He heard the still waiting; sensed the cramping of muscles, the wriggling, weary children; shuddered at the dim whine of the sick and injured. And then the smoke, filtering slowly, then more rapidly along the gallery, cloudy whorls spiralling up to the invisible ceiling and drifting slowly back downwards, great bowls of smoke wafting into the minute spaces between the living beings.

'Menouira,' the professor called sharply, focusing again on the now-distant button of light, '*Ça suffit*. Enough.'

On the walk back, too, Menouira led the way. The distance which had seemed so great was now a matter of a hundred metres, the surprised O of the sky widening with each step.

Not far from the exit, the professor stumbled over something. He reached down and pulled up a long, narrow object, slimed with mud. Menouira held the torch beside him, and he did his best to wipe the thing clean, but he knew before he had exposed its ivory cast, before even it saw the light, that he held a bone.

'I believe,' he said, handing it to Menouira for inspection, 'that this is a human femur.'

Menouira took the bone and turned it in his hand. Without a word, he raised his arm and hurled it back into the darkness, where they heard its dull clatter against the wall of the cave, and the sucking thud as it settled back into the *oued*.

Only when the afternoon breeze swept upon his face and dried his tears did the professor realize that he had been crying.

Progress with three mules proved slower than with two, and the professor's crossing to Rabelais came to seem interminable. Hour after hour, the animal beneath him jangled his limbs and assaulted his spine, kicking up dust until his suit was wholly pink.

Ibrahim no longer waved his switch at the mules: he kept his eyes to the ground which, as they climbed higher, grew more unyielding. Mustafa strode several paces ahead, eyeing the landscape warily, scanning the horizon and the hills for movement. When they stopped, the two men from Cassaigne did not smile and made no attempt to converse with the professor. They spoke quietly to each other, almost furtively, and they ate their meals with their bodies hunched over upon themselves.

The professor was made nervous, but did not show it. Self-control was, he knew, the source of authority. But sometimes, as they jolted forwards, his stomach would leap. He wondered if uncle and nephew planned to murder him in the mountain pass, to abandon his corpse to the hyenas, and to return, in haste and with their extra mule, to Cassaigne. The Oriental character, he knew from his research—and from his experience with Menouira in the cave—was alien to his own. The compassion, the civilized impulse, was not there. Menouira had walked the length of the sepulchre where his ancestors had been massacred, and felt nothing. The Ouled Riah could live without revulsion under the rule of the *caid*. What, to such people, was the life of the professor? They did not see the necessity of his work: history, too, meant nothing to them.

When they stopped to camp for the night, by the edge of an *oued* between two crests, the professor withdrew from the fire, and unbuckled his case. He took from it, surreptitiously, the wallet that held his money, and stuffed it against his belly, beneath his shirt, tucked into the waistband of his trousers. In this way he felt protected, somewhat, from the danger he imagined he now saw in Mustafa's gaze, in the way his delicate fingers plucked at his beard.

In the night, the professor woke to see Mustafa still seated by the fire, watching him and smoking. Conjuring a flicker of menace in the Arab's eye, he felt for the wallet, his wealth resting, like his name, against him.

'Do you not sleep?' he asked, in Arabic.

'I will sleep tomorrow night,' said Mustafa. 'When we reach Rabelais.'

The professor closed his eyes again, and dreamt of his own murder.

Rabelais was a larger town, and merited a French administrator, who welcomed his bedraggled compatriot with enthusiasm. He was a tall, square man with a round, lined face, and he clapped the professor on the back, causing small puffs of coloured dust to whisk about them. Ushering him into the tiled domain, he offered him a bed and a hot bath, and hospitality for as long as the professor cared to stay. He also offered a cigar, which the professor smoked luxuriantly, seated, filthy as he was, in a soft chair in the administrator's office.

Through the window, he could see Mustafa and Ibrahim watering their animals at the fountain in the cobbled square, waiting for his instructions. The professor was overcome by annoyance at the two men from Cassaigne whom he believed had cast such doubt on his mission. Their busied forms were reproachful, and he wanted them gone.

He excused himself from the administrator's office and, cigar in hand, called to Mustafa from the steps of the government building. The French flag snapped and billowed above his head. Pulling the wallet at last from his belt, he counted out half again as much as they had agreed, a thick wad of notes, and pronounced them free to go.

He was not a man to feel absurd, and it did not occur to him that he looked odd, beneath the flag, his clothes grimy, his glasses slightly askew; nor that it was strange to grant freedom to two free men.

'I wish you a safe journey,' he offered, magnanimous.

'*Inch'allah*,' murmured uncle and nephew in unison.

'We wish you luck with your history,' called Mustafa, as the two men turned towards the narrow Arab streets at the edge of the square. The professor could have sworn he caught a smile quivering, insolent, in the Arab's beard.

The administrator, although he had been a decade in Rabelais, had no knowledge of the caves of the Sbéhas. He had not visited them, and showed only a bemused interest.

'I think you are mistaken,' he repeated several times. 'The *enfumade*—a great tragedy—befell the Ouled Riah, near Necmaria. That is the cave you should visit. Not that there could be anything particular to see.'

28

'I have been to Necmaria. I've just come from here. I want to see the caves of the Sbéhas. Was he then Colonel Saint-Arnaud not stationed near here in forty-five?'

'Perhaps,' said the administrator. He offered his guest another glass of local wine, holding his ruby glass to the light. 'You might think it was from home, no? The viticulture is improving so rapidly.'

He, too, to the professor's irritation, saw little point in the expedition. 'Even if there was such an accident, it is best forgotten, surely?' he asked with a smile, his lips disappearing among the lines of his face. 'Who wants to remember? In France, there is a war on: morale is of the essence. Who would wish to know about such a disgrace? These things are accidents of war; and our attention must be on the accidents at hand. I hear they are sending our boys to the front in taxis. May God save Paris from the Boche! Persistent buggers. Uncivilized.'

Washed and changed, the professor became again his unflappable, urbane self. He sat in the

comfort of the administrator's drawing-room, h
head against an antimacassar crocheted b
Monsieur's charming wife. He opened th
Colonel's letters, a leatherbound volume that b
had carried with him from the city, all that wa
and in which he had marked the relevant page
He read again the correspondence from Sain
Arnaud to his brother, dated 15 August, 1845:

The same day, the 8th, I sent a reconnaissance to
the grottos, or rather, caverns. We were met by
gunfire, and I was so surprised that I respectfully
saluted several shots, which is not my habit. The
same evening, the 53rd came under enemy fire,
one man wounded, measures well taken. The
9th, the beginnings of the work of siege: *blocus*,
mines, grenades, summations, instances, entreaties
that they should emerge and surrender. Answer:
insults, blasphemies, shots fired. 10th, 11th, more
of the same. So, on the 12th, I had all the exits
hermetically sealed, and I made of the cave a vast
cemetery. The earth will cover for-ever the corpses
of these fanatics. Nobody went into the caves—

no one . . . only I know that interred therein are
500 brigands who will no longer slit French
throats. A confidential report told the command-
er-in-chief everything, simply, without terrible
poetry and without descriptions.

Brother, nobody is good by taste and nature
as I am. From the 8th to the 12th I was sickened,
but I have a clear conscience. I did my duty as a
leader, and tomorrow I will begin again. But I
have taken Africa in disgust—and am taken with
disgust for Africa.

The professor closed the book and wiped his
lasses. He had found no record anywhere of the
onfidential report, and no mention was made of
he event in histories of the campaign. But the
rofessor believed. He closed his eyes and smelt
gain the cave at Necmaria, the air of death, and
e was certain that Saint-Arnaud had not lied to
is brother. The secrecy had been his military
iumph: the deaths, expedient, had furthered the
attle, and the dead could not speak.

'Perhaps I could speak to the locals?' he

suggested over supper, served at the administra
tor's oval dining table, brought by boat and trai
from France and carrying with it the heavy sme
of French polish.

'Perhaps,' said the administrator's wife, wh
spoke little and, when she did, waved her plump
pale hands like mittens in the air. 'Perhaps th
professor should consult our hermit.'

The administrator emitted a jolly snort an
slapped the professor's forearm on the tabl
'Naim will take you to the hermit. If you fin
nothing else, he, at least, will provide a subject fo
study.'

'What sort of hermit is he?' asked the profe
sor, gingerly retrieving his arm from the admini
trator's grasp.

'Up in the hills,' said the wife, 'we have a he
mit. A count, no less, and a very extraordina
man. He has wandered the desert for—how lon
mon cher?'

'Decades.' The administrator gulped his win
'He is, indeed, a man of God, ordained by . . .
forget by whom. But our church doesn't seem t

be a priority. He doesn't preach, or even venture very often into Rabelais. He seems to prefer the company of natives, although I don't believe he has any intention of converting them. He has been known to deliver the Muslim prayers for the dying when the need arises. A sideline as an *imam*, if you like.'

'I like him,' said the wife. 'He's a gentle man, and has taken the time to listen to these miserable people. They trust him. Whereas with us'—she fluttered her hands, a glinting implement in each this time—'who can say? I don't like to be here when my husband goes away, because their faces . . . their eyes . . . you do not know.'

'They carry the history we have forgotten,' said the professor. 'Our beginnings here were brutal.'

'They have no interest in history,' said the administrator. 'The past to them is like their soil in summer, scattered on the wind. At Necmaria, you know, the *caid* is descended not from the Ouled Riah, over whom he rules, but from their enemies. And they don't know it, or care. Like dust, it's gone.'

'They know,' countered the professor, with new understanding born simply of dislike of the administrator. 'And they won't ever forget. They live in front of their defeat, and it is always with them. But they're different from us. They know what is necessary for survival.'

'And they will use it when they can,' said the wife, sombre now. 'Don't think, *mon cher*, that they won't. They harbour it like a seed, and nurture it in secret. One day, we will all pay.'

'This is why the stories must be told,' said the professor, eager yet again to convey his vital purpose. 'There is a war in Europe now. We must learn from the past before mistakes are made. Do you see? For the progress of France, here and at home, the truth must be known. Knowledge . . .' he stammered, flushed from the wine and conviction, 'knowledge is the only salvation. For the past and the future both.'

'Noble sentiments indeed,' said the administrator. 'But I suspect you have only the experience of your library. Forgive me, but I speak as a former military man, and I can assure you, the maps of old battles are of very little use in the field. Wits and courage are what's called for: the rest is a waste and a distraction.'

The professor did not respond.

'Tell me, what good is it? What difference will it make, to tell your story, even if it is true?'

This time, the professor did not bother to try.

Naim, the administrator's steward, took the professor up into the hills. They walked for two hours, Rabelais reduced behind them to a silent hive, its French quarter invisible in the lacy comb of native houses.

The hermit's encampment, though remote, had a clear view of the town. The clay of the one-room building was weathered and covered, in places, by creepers, and in front stretched an area of ground trampled flat and even as a floor. Outside the doorway waited a neat pile of firewood. There did not, at first, appear to be anyone at home, and Naim beat his staff against the ground and called out in Arabic.

Two figures emerged from along a path that ran behind the building: a surprising sight. In front walked the hermit, a towering, skeletally thin man with attenuated limbs that stretched, puppet-like, from the cuffs and hem of his gown. His skin was so browned by the sun and his coarse garments were so ragged that initially only his shock of silvered hair confirmed his European breeding. A closer inspection revealed his patrician profile and his pale blue eyes, and the rich timbre of his French voice when he spoke left no room for doubt.

Behind him loomed an immense black African, powerfully muscled and clad in equally ill-fitting clothes. He was introduced as Kofeh, the hermit's assistant of long standing. He did not stay to talk with them, but returned to his work, skinning the sheep a local tribe had donated for their food.

Naim and the hermit spoke for some time in Arabic, about Naim's relatives and the birth of his third child. The hermit conversed in Naim's language as readily as in French, and the two spoke to each other as friends, without any lingering reserve. The hermit asked after other families in Rabelais, but he did not mention the administrator until he turned and spoke in French to the professor.

'How is our good friend, the standard-bearer of French glory?' he asked. 'Do you know, he does not allow Kofeh into his drawing-room, and so I can't visit him often. I am partial, however, to his wife; and when he is called to the city, I try to stop in on her. They have no children. She is very alone in that house.'

'I can imagine,' said the professor. 'She appears to have a nervous disposition. But I found her most sympathetic—it was she who suggested I consult you. You've lived a long time among these people, and I thought you would know of their history.'

'I know a little.'

'I wish to write a book. In seventy years, no one has told the truth about our campaigns in this region.'

'That may be.'

'The cave at Necmaria, from which I have recently travelled . . . I believe it is not the only cross we have to bear. Here, too . . .'

'Yes, here, too.'

'You know, then, about the *enfumade* of the Sbéhas?'

'It is spoken of. Those French who acknowledge it speak only of a handful of brigands. You won't find any Frenchman who can tell you the story. Saint-Arnaud covered his tracks well, and who would wish to expose them? The lesson they leave, next to Necmaria, is that of a job well done. Not an agreeable lesson, but a useful one: if you want to succeed, kill them all. Leave nobody alive who can speak. It is a lesson I fear that mankind—even European men—should not learn too well. Because none of us is civilized enough. Even, and perhaps especially, to the enlightened, extermination is not a lesson to be taught.'

'There were no survivors then?'

'Maybe that is what is to be gleaned. There are always survivors.'

'Where can I hear more?'

The hermit looked to Naim, who frowned.

'Will you not?' the hermit asked, his face coaxing, his eyebrows slightly raised.

Naim spoke without looking at the professor. 'My grandfather was one of those in the cave who survived. He was only a small boy. You walked on the corpses as on piles of hay,' he said. 'The cave is an underground *oued*, on two levels. Only those in the upper chamber had any hope of survival. At both ends, the cave is entered through waterfalls: the French did not only smoke them in, they cemented the exits, and camped, two weeks almost, outside, so no rescue could be attempted. The dead gave off gases, purulent rot, poison. And the water which kept the few alive ran beneath their decomposing bodies. My grandfather thought that he, too, had died: his mind was deranged. When at last he saw the light again, he believed he was in heaven, and that the men who helped him through the curtain of water to the air were his brothers and cousins, the very

39

ones who had lain, homes to feasting maggots, in the mud beneath his feet.'

'How did they get to safety?' asked the professor, the memory of Necmaria vivid in his mind. 'Did the troops relent?'

'It is said,' said Naim, 'that a *caid* from a neighbouring region prevailed, finally, upon the commander. That he was desperate to see again the most beautiful woman in the mountains, whom he had planned to marry. And that he was determined to have her, alive or dead. The commander, it seems, who showed no mercy to a thousand of his fellows, understood the love of a woman and permitted the opening of the cave.'

'And the dead?'

'She was among them, but the *caid* did not take her away after all. Her face had pulled back upon itself, the skin and the eyes were gone. He knew her only by the length of her hair and the gold around her neck and fingers. He left her there, and all the others. The cave was their tomb.'

Kofeh, at this point, returned from behind the house, bringing tea. The story was at an end.

'My heart is confused,' said the hermit to the professor, 'when I hear of our legacy. What is the purpose of such violence? And yet, how else would I be here?' He paused to drink. 'Must we believe that this is the will of God? Or does our life's struggle pass unheeded in heaven? I have no answer.'

'Do you see that I must tell this story?' asked the professor, believing that he had found at last a man of vision and justice.

'I see that this is your struggle,' said the hermit. 'It is with you, and with God.'

Back in the city, the professor compiled his notes. Weeks, and then months passed. The days in the mountains of Dahra stood out from his life like the plain in front of the mountains, hazed in the light, an unreachable promise. The library where he worked was still and dark, its high windows and thick walls a silent, stifling enclosure against the contradictions of the country. The call of the *muezzin* reached his ears only as a muffled wail, the keeper of ritual and the passage of time.

For the first time in his many years of study, the professor was uneasy about his work. Even were he to finish his book, who would read it? It was not clear that this was a time for truth: extermination was not a lesson that the people needed to learn. But what might be the consequences of silence?

Eventually, he forsook the library for the clamour of the port, where the men worked bare-chested, heaving and shouting as the ships were docked and unloaded. He wandered, too, in the maze of the kasbah, among the hot perfumes of spice and dung. Even the bustling, bourgeois arcades of his compatriots were preferable to the silence of the library. He neglected his students as well as his work: he sought in the city the truth of the mountains, the air of the caves catching him, here and there, in gusts.

He learned that his nephew—only a boy when he had seen him last—had been killed at the front, in a battle over a patch of wet ground north of Paris. He learned, too, not long after, that the hermit of Rabelais and his hulking disciple had been slain in their sleep, their throats slit in crimson grins that neither Kofeh's strength nor the hermit's gentle patience could close up again. The newspaper made much of the hermit's noble birth, and the end of his lineage, of the fact that an ancient castle in south-western France would now pass into the hands of strangers. The professor could see only the small building, alone on the plateau in the Dahra, crumbling again to dust, its firewood standing unused in a neat pile; and the town of Rabelais far below, living on, oblivious.

Long before he had even planned his excursion, before these stories had begun to consume him, the professor had discovered, within the safety of the library itself, mementoes of his ancestors' conquest. Unable to confront this horror, he had chosen to ignore it: it had been as easy as shutting a drawer. But now, troubled, he returned to the library. There, carefully stored in a cupboard in the corner, was a large jar of th liquid, in which swam a swarm of pinkish shrimp-like creatures. These perfect curls, some still trailing strands of hair, no two quite alike, were the preserved ears of native rebels, claimed by the French as a warning and a marker in the early days of the colony. For seventy or more years they had floated in their brine, waiting, listening for something unheard. For them, the professor decided at last, if only to them, he would tell his story.